mopqrsuvwxyz

for le baugni, louis and rémi.

Translated from the French by Julie Harris with Lory Frankel

Project Coordinator, English-language edition: Ellen Cohen

Editor, English-language edition: Lory Frankel

ISBN 0-8109-1245-7

Copyright © 1996 Éditions du Seuil, Paris

English-language edition copyright © 1997 Harry N. Abrams, Inc.

Published in 1997 by Harry N. Abrams, Incorporated, New York

A Times Mirror Company

Printed and bound in Belgium

The Boy Who Ate Words

by Thierry Dedieu

Harry N. Abrams, Inc., Publishers

One day, a little boy stopped talking.

His name was Anthony the Gabber, or Gabby for short.

In the beginning, Gabby was just like any other child. Nothing set him apart from other little boys his age. Like all little boys, he would rather dump all his toys on the floor than clean up his room. Like all little boys, he would rather eat spaghetti than peas. Like all little boys, he liked sweets more than spinach.

He had been just like all the rest.

He had wanted to know everything, to understand everything. As soon as he learned how to talk, he asked millions of questions.

"When are we eating?"

"Why do houses have roofs?"

"Who put all the fish in the water?"

"Why do trees grow *up*?"

"Who? What? Where? When? How?"

He looked at the world through a forest of question marks.

When he wasn't asking questions, Gabby started guessing, or he gave explanations, and invented solutions. All the time, he talked. Talked and talked.

It wasn't easy for his mother.

It wasn't easy for his father.

Ideas crossed each other in Gabby's head. As he was speaking of one thing, the idea of another came to him. Ideas that hatched, grew big, and waited at the gates of his lips. All this jumbled together in his mouth. It kicked up a commotion. And, of course, it put him out of commission.

When the ideas came out, it was impossible to understand him. He didn't separate his words anymore. Everything got tied together in one long string. This produced phrases like:

TheballoonisdeflatedbecausetomorrowisWednesday.

There'snomoremilkinmyschoolbag.

Waswhywhogotchocolateonmyapron?

??

He created a language of his own. Gabby spoke "Gabby."

His parents were very worried. It was impossible to have a conversation with him. His mother asked him to pronounce all his words clearly, to sep-a-rate all the syl-la-bles. But nothing worked. It was worse than trying to understand Chinese!

One day, his parents, exasperated, told him they wouldn't speak to him anymore if he continued to swallow all his words.

For Gabby, this was a revelation. Of course, that was it! Some people drank water, chewed gum, or sucked on chicken bones, while he . . . he ate words.

And he found his taste for words grew stronger.

Of course, he needed to live on cheese and meat and vegetables, but he also began to live on verbs and pronouns.

He listened and then repeated the words that seemed the most delicious.

"Whipped cream strawberry pizza spaghetti," or "Chicken vanilla" . . .

But, quickly, other words satisfied him: "locomotive" and "hair curler." He preferred nice round, chubby words. Some words upset him; the word "taxi" made him cough. He spit it out immediately. It was the same thing for "cupcake" or "tarantula."

Gabby learned how to read, or at least how to recognize the shapes of words. He opened a book to any page and selected his menu.

For the first course, he chose little words: "before, here, yes, not a lot."

For the main dish, he chose words with a little more meat on them: "gargoyle," "administered," or "neighborhood." He liked best words with a sauce: *on the other side of the* bridge," "*across from the* station."

Finally, for dessert, he treated himself to sweets – "cabinet" topped with a "pumpkin," like the cherry on a sundae.

Gabby ate greedily. Without chewing. He devoured his food rather than savor it. When he said "cabinet-pumpkin," others only heard "cabin."

It was pleasing to Gabby, but impossible for others to understand.

Above all, instead of sampling bits and pieces here and there and keeping himself from eating between reading out loud, he nibbled, nonstop. Gulping down a word from a poster in the street here, snatching an adjective in a magazine title there, sucking on a description elsewhere. . . .

So one fine day, he got indigestion. Nothing came out anymore, not even an exclamation. Oh dear! Nothing.

Queasy, he fell to his knees and threw up two or three consonants.

After putting him to bed, his panic-stricken parents called the doctor. The doctor listened to Gabby's chest and looked at his throat and made him say: 10 and 1, 10 and 1. Gabby repeated, "Tender thumb, tender thumb." The doctor quickly removed his hand from the child's mouth. He decided that Gabby's problem was that he ate too much. His parents were surprised by this diagnosis; their child seemed to eat just the right amount. Though they had their doubts, they followed the doctor's advice and put Gabby on a diet. Being a good child, he went along with it.

From then on, Gabby would be very careful.

His parents paid attention to what he ate, and Gabby paid attention to what he said. He was content in the morning to say the date on the calendar, accompanied by two or three remarks about the weather, and then rush off to school feeling hungry.

No more repeating the roll call during recess. No more snacking on a page from a magazine after school.

His diet was a strict one, but it soon paid off. Gabby began to be understood. Speaking more slowly and using fewer words meant that he began to separate his syllables – to the great relief of his parents. But for him, it was only frustrating. All that he had in his head, all his ideas, his questions – could not be expressed with so few words.

What was the good of asking, "How is the weather?", when deep, deep down inside, what one really wanted to know was: "How are clouds born? What makes the rain? Why does the sun shine only during the day?"

So Gabby went on a kind of hunger strike. He completely stopped talking.

His parents called the doctor back. Gabby opened his mouth wide. There was nothing strange to be found. His speech organs were fine. They thought perhaps he was deaf. Gabby opened his ears wide. His hearing organs were fine.

They had to accept the truth. Gabby was silent because he wanted to be silent.

This is how he responded when his mother asked him what he did at school that day:

"...

...."

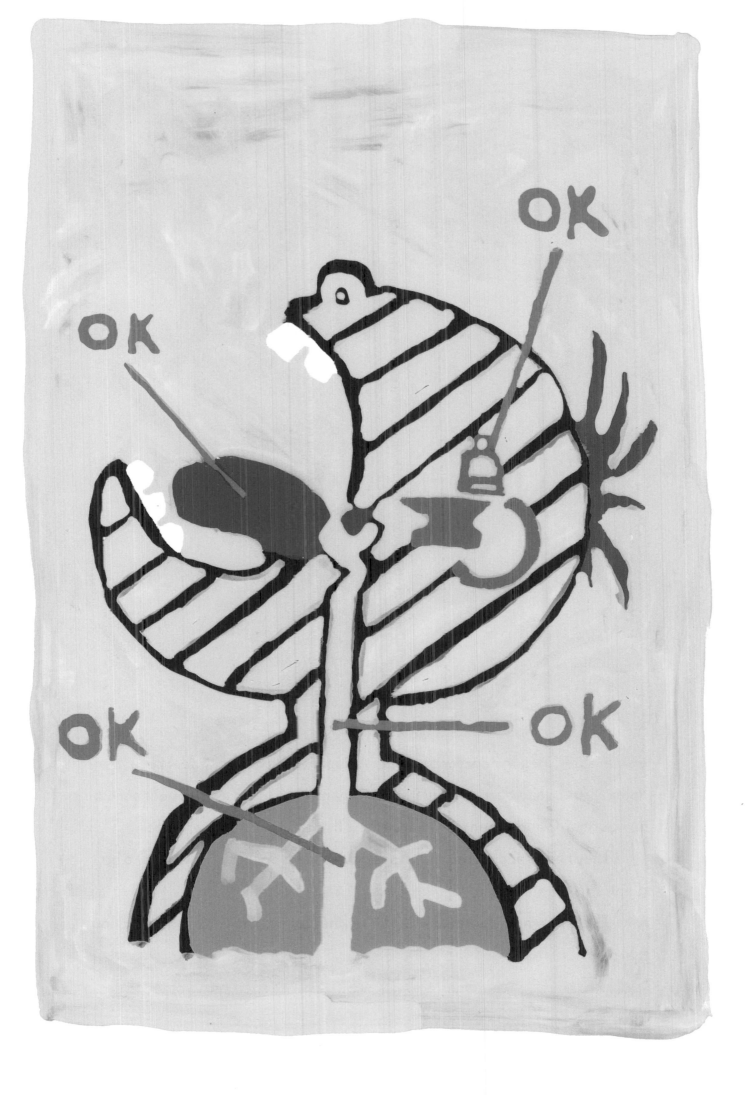

Even though he didn't speak anymore, Gabby hadn't stopped thinking, watching, feeling, and experiencing. So in order to be understood without a word, he used his nose, his hands, his skin, his gaze – everything to help him discover and understand the world around him.

One day, while he was in his room, in the middle of getting dressed to go out, his cat said to him, "Don't forget your boots and your raincoat; it's going to rain." Gabby thanked him for his advice, and dressed accordingly.

The cat had obviously not made a sound, but the exchange had, indeed, taken place. The cat had scratched behind his ear to warn Gabby about the thunderstorm, and Gabby had thanked him with the wink of an eye.

Gabby made great strides communicating.

Body language turned out to be more expressive than all the words humans use. His expression alone could signal hundreds of emotions (doubt, joy, pain, weariness, fear, excitement...).

And his hands! They made a fist, froze, gripped, caressed, trembled, sweat, hit, waved...

This new vocabulary made it possible for Gabby to express several feelings at the same time. A fit of the shivers, a raised eyebrow, a wrinkled forehead, a pointed finger, a hand that brushed the surface lightly, lips that pouted, then curved into the slightest suggestion of a smile...

He learned to express himself with his entire body.

Animals were his best teachers.

From dogs he learned what can be said with the ears, the nose, and facial expressions. Certain gestures meant "I'll do what you want" or "You'll do what I want."

From cats, he learned what can be said with fur. He learned lessons in wisdom and meditation, how to be quick when necessary, and how to keep calm the rest of the time. Patience. Cunning. Determination. Independence.

With a little help from his friends, Gabby explored other, more fleeting languages.

The language of flowers, for example. He talked for hours with the daisies, listened to the gladioli tell him stories about their wild youth among the dandelions.

It was wonderful. He loved that. You could tell.

Gabby also spoke rather unusual languages, like the language of the "statue" in the public gardens, or the "dictionary" in the library, or even the "furniture" language used by chairs, tables, and cupboards.... He had laughing fits with the handsaw, shouting matches with the kitchen stool, and he even learned things from the front door!

His parents were worried. They felt this wasn't normal. They decided to send Gabby to a "home." It was a special place where he would find other children like himself.

When Gabby entered the huge hall where they were all gathered together, he was welcomed with a deafening silence.

Not one word was spoken, but they all, in their own languages, said hello to Gabby, who in turn introduced himself in "ant" language. With a few jerky movements, countless flutterings of his eyelashes, two kicks and one step backward, he said that his name was Gabby, that he was pleased to meet them.

He said he was sure that he would get on well with them.

It turned out that it wasn't so easy communicating with the other children. The children knew too many ways to express themselves.

One could use the "flower" language, and the other would respond in "cat," following up with explanations in "furniture." This meant he had to pay attention at all times to their slightest signals.

When the speaker scratched himself, for example, that could mean, depending on the language used: "I prefer milk," or "I'm going for a run in the field," or "I have something to do in the afternoon."

The days went by and Gabby got used to his new life. Until something happened that suddenly turned his world upside down.

That something was named Lola.

Lola was the caretaker's daughter. Gabby had always thought her to be just like all the other children.

But one day, he discovered that Lola spoke "human." She spoke in a voice so gentle, so musical that Gabby was filled with admiration. From her mouth fell words so harmonious that it actually made him want to take up the strained and narrow language once again. It must be said that when Lola spoke, it was . . .

It was fine.

When she said, "I like the color orange," one understood, "Of all the colors, the one I find the most dazzling is the color of the sun that dives into the sea, the color of the sweet fruit from the land of a thousand and one nights that quenches the thirst of the wanderer, tired and worn from a long voyage."

It was fine.

It was sweet as honey.

At first, Gabby tried to communicate with Lola, to make her see that he wanted to be her friend. Once, Gabby left her scented messages, the way moths do, on the windowsills and door handles. The effect was disastrous. From then on, whenever she bumped into him, she held her nose.

Then Gabby adopted the language of ironing. With the help of some handkerchiefs, he folded them cleverly so that they looked like animals. And so Lola often found, either on her chair or her desk, a piece of fabric folded in the shape of a frog or a rabbit.

But still the message was not clear. Gabby had to face the truth. Lola didn't understand anything apart from human language.

After taking a long time to think it over, Gabby resolved to use human words once again. But he would be very strict in selecting them. He would choose his words carefully for their harmony, their meaning, their color, for the movement of his lips.

So that each word pronounced would not be just one more word in the hubbub made by humans. So that it would be like a diamond he would offer to someone who knew how to listen to it.

And, just as Gabby was preparing himself to utter his first precious word, Lola handed him a word made of paper.